Written by Gaby Goldsack
Illustrated by Steve Smallman

This edition published by Parragon in 2008

Parragon
Queen Street House
4 Queen Street
Bath BA1 1HE, UK

ISBN 978-1-4075-3169-4

Muddy Puddle

Illustrated by Steve Smallman

Bath · New York · Singapore · Hong Kong · Cologne · Delhi · Melbourne

It was a sunny day on the farm. The animals were hot and thirsty. Farmer Fred whistled cheerily as he carried his pail to the water faucet.

Farmer Fred turned on the faucet. It whistled and clanked, but no water came out. He turned on every faucet in the barnyard, but not a drop of water came out.

"I don't believe it," he called to his wife, Jenny. "There's no water!"

"I'll go and phone the Water Company," said Jenny.

Meanwhile, Patch the Sheepdog set off to check on the sheep. But as he passed Hog Hollow, he heard a grunting noise.

"My muddy puddle has dried up," Polly Pig complained. "If I don't get a mud bath soon I'm sure to get sunburned."

"I'll fetch Farmer Fred," barked Patch. "He'll think of something."

"Trembling tomatoes!" cried Farmer Fred when he saw Polly Pig. "We need to make a mud bath. But there's no water in the faucets."

Just then, he heard Dotty Duck quacking.

"I've an idea!" said Farmer Fred. He picked up his pail and began to fill it with water from the duck pond.

"Quack, quack!" cried Dotty Duck crossly. There was hardly enough water left for the ducks to swim.

"Hmm, I'll get water from the creek instead," decided Farmer Fred.

Farmer Fred fetched two pails of water from the creek, and carried them back to Hog Hollow. He tipped them into Polly's dried up muddy patch, and then went to fetch some more.

Up and down, up and down he went. But when he stopped for a rest, he couldn't believe his eyes. Hog Hollow was as dry as ever!

"Bouncing boots! It's drying up faster than I can fill it!" cried Farmer Fred.

"Well, perhaps Harry Horse can help," thought Farmer Fred. But when Farmer Fred fixed two pails over Harry's back, he simply dug in his hoofs and refused to budge.

"Neigh! Neigh!" he complained. It was far too hot to work.

"Oh, dear," said Farmer Fred, fanning Polly with his hat. "How are we going to make you a mud bath?"

Never fear, I've an idea!

Just then, he spotted a length
of hosepipe curled up beside
the milking parlor.

"Never fear!" he cried, "I've an
idea!" And, grabbing the hosepipe,
he raced back to his workshop.

Farmer Fred bashed and crashed around inside his workshop.

Before long, the door to the workshop swung open. The animals stood back as Farmer Fred pushed out a strange machine with the hose attached.

"This," explained Farmer Fred,
"is a pump-action, sun-powered Puddle
Filler. We'll soon have the biggest mud
bath you have ever seen."

The animals followed Farmer Fred at a safe distance as he pushed the Puddle Filler down to the creek.

"Whatever is he up to now?" neighed Harry Horse, shaking his head.

Everyone held their breath as Farmer Fred flipped a switch on the Puddle Filler. It spluttered into life.

"Now, just wait for the water," cried Farmer Fred. But nothing happened. No water appeared. Not one drop.

"Ah! The hose must be blocked," said Farmer Fred, peering down its end.

Suddenly, the hose began to hiss and squirm.

"Popping parsnips!" cried Farmer Fred, as the Puddle Filler reared up and chased him around Hog Hollow. Everyone scattered as it snaked and flapped this way and that.

Farmer Fred landed with a bump next to Polly Pig.

"It doesn't look like you'll be getting your mud bath after all!" he said. Then, Farmer Fred felt a drip fall on his head.

"Hurray, it's raining!" he cried, and burst into song...

"Woof, woof," barked Patch, looking up at the tree above the pigsty. Farmer Fred looked up. It wasn't raining. The hose was stuck in the tree and a cool shower was falling over Hog Hollow.

Just then, Jenny appeared at Hog Hollow with some good news.

"The Water Company said there was a burst pipe. It's fixed now, so the faucets should be working."

At that moment, water gushed from all the faucets in the barnyard. Before long, Polly, Patch and the other animals were jumping in all the muddy puddles.

"It never rains but it pours," laughed Farmer Fred.